Once Upon a Pond

A. B. Guthrie, Jr.

Illustrated by Carol B. Guthrie

MOUNTAIN PRESS PUBLISHING COMPANY
Missoula, Montana

MOUNTAIN PRESS PUBLISHING COMPANY

287 West Front Street

Missoula, Montana 59801

To Mary Helen, Helen, Bert, Amy, Billie, Kelly, Tommie and all the little people, some not so little now, who have enjoyed versions of these tales and hoped some day to see them in print. I must add that but for the faith and perseverance of the illustrator, who didn't think she could illustrate them, they wouldn't be in print yet.

Contents

An Invitation

Pond Placid is a place I know,
And, if you want to, there we'll go
To call upon wise Cousin Frog
And Busy Beaver with his log,
Mephitis Skunk and Scissorbill.
They'll be there still.
They'll be there still.

Amphibious Turtle, take his name.
For Mousie Muskrat do the same.
Put Mollie Cottontail down then —
All friends of mine from way back when.
Let's go then, believing, go with care.
They'll still be there.
They'll still be there.

Count Ursa Minor, if in reach,
That bear with trouble in his speech;
And Maggie with her magpie's call
Who cries, "Assemble, one and all!"
So softly now. Old memory
Begins to hear, begins to see.
And here at last are we.

Hello, There

Over Pond Placid, over the length and breadth of it and beyond its shores, sounded the harsh voice of Maggie Magpie, who was the pond crier and would cry out nothings when there was nothing to cry.

"Hurrah for spring!" she was shouting now. "Hail, leaf and bud! Out of your beds and burrows, everyone! Out of your winter snooze! Awake!" It didn't matter to her that everyone was awake.

Flying, she could see all of Pond Placid, from the beaver dam that made it, thanks to Busy Beaver, to the thread of stream that fed it. On both shores grew willows and cottonwoods and chokecherry and serviceberry bushes and clean clumps of aspen, all in first leaf now, tinted with that brave, beginning color that artists call an acid green. A snug place, she thought, well hidden from the world. And indeed it was, though she knew nothing about the world that lay outside a four-mile circle centered by the pond. Not knowing, she could not have said that Pond Placid nestled in a pocket of the eastern apron of the Rocky Mountains far from the great ant hills of men.

"Salute, salute the happy time!"

Under Maggie, who knew her world by heart, was Busy Beaver's house, hard by the shore. Scissorbill Eagle, the King of Birds, was perched high on a cliff to the west, close to the nest his wife was building. Maggie didn't expect even a hello flap of the wing from him, his pride was so high. Mollie Cottontail, an evening feeder, wasn't in sight. Neither were Mephitis Skunk and his wife. Mephitis was probably ambling along in the underbrush, made more than ever cheerful by the thought of finding an early-laid egg for his lunch. The Tommy Chipmunks were scurrying about as usual, up bush and tree, down bush and tree and on the mending ground, their tails flirting like tiny, secret signals. Mousie Muskrat had his nervous nose poked from the water beside his reed house

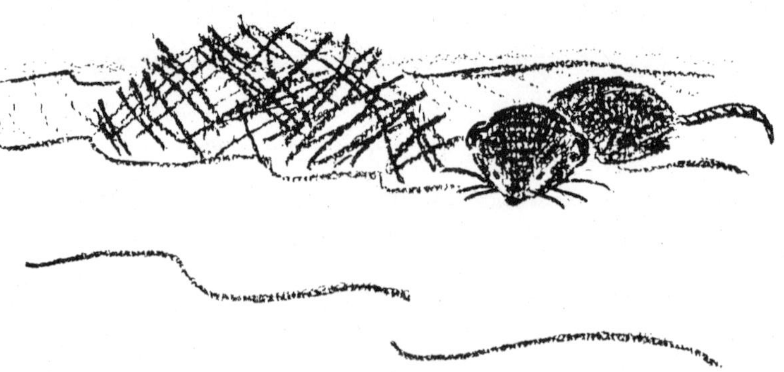

in the shallows. He pulled it half in as Maggie's shadow passed and then lifted an uncertain paw by way of greeting. Then her eyes picked up Cousin Frog and Amphibious Turtle on the lip of the eastern shore, as still as fallen, unblown leaves.

"Hail to the glad time, brain and babe," Maggie screeched at them. "Spring warms cold blood. Or should!"

Amphibious stirred from his half-drowse and asked Cousin Frog, "What's all the shouting about?"

"Hush," Cousin Frog answered. He still felt sluggish from his winter's sleep and warmed but a little by the sun, and his mind searched for himself in what he'd been and known before this waking up. "Now is the remembering time."

"I don't remember much," Amphibious said. "I don't remember anything." He was a very small turtle, not so large as the palm of a child's hand.

"Persons who remember what they never have known are quite rare," Cousin Frog told him. "But time will take care of you, time and I. We will see to your head."

For himself Cousin Frog remembered when Pond Placid was no more than a streamlet and he a small frog just shed of his tadpole's tail who couldn't hop as high as a grass stem. Then the Beavers had come, Busy and Missus, and with log and branch and puddled mud had dammed the stream and made the pond. Afterwards others arrived, water people and land people, fur and feathers, hide and horn, all drawn to the still reservoir.

Constantly after the dam was built, Busy still tended it, sealing over its leaks, adding branches and mud and sometimes a

log to places that showed the least signs of weakness. He deserved his nickname, all right, even though, just last summer, he had started making up verses, having learned something of meters and rhymes from Cousin Frog himself. Sometimes now he would cease work, spit out a mouthful of chips and recite a jingle that pleased him.

At last the sun had warmed Cousin Frog, and he left off remembering. "Soon comes the time of things happening," he told Amphibious.

"What makes things happen, Cousin Frog?"

Cousin Frog gave thought to the question and at last answered. "Things. Things bring on things."

He didn't know how right he was. Even as he spoke it seemed to him he heard, far off, a whispered rumble like thunder worlds away.

It was the first of things.

Nature's Faces

Traitor Nature, shall we call her,
Counting drouth or violent water,
Coming just as days were good
And she'd acted as she should,
Counting fun brought to an end
After we had called her friend?

One thing, wrongful, is the case:
Nature loves to change her face.
Just as leaf and life come out,
Watch out for a turn-about!
Watch for rain or flood that say
Come again another day.

Blast you, Nature, wipe your frown!
Think Pond Placid wants to drown?

The Flood
Like None Before

Cousin Frog was worried. The thunder he had thought he heard he heard undoubtedly now. It was the thunder of water, the roar of flood. Already, though the high tide of the creek was an approaching sound and not yet a presence, the pond was uneasy. And from sunup to high sun it had risen so much that Mousie Muskrat's house barely poked from the surface.

He told himself that everyone would live through high water, inconvenient as it might be to some. He and Amphibious could keep edging up the bank so's always to be on the last lip of the waves. The Muskrats, already drowned out, still would survive, afloat or ashore. The Busy Beavers, if they had to, would make burrows somewhere in a dry bank. The Chipmunks would take to the tracery of the trees. Mephitis Skunk's house was above any likely flood level. And Maggie and the Eagles had no cause for concern.

But what if, under the tear of water, the dam went out! In his mind's eye Cousin Frog saw Pond Placid not a pond any more but a dried, mud-cracked waste where thickets were sprouting.

And there was not a thing he could do. He wasn't made for the labor that would help make the dam fast. He was made for thought, if for anything, and not a thought he could think would hold back the tide.

He said to Amphibious, "See you."

"Why are you angry with me, Cousin Frog?"

Cousin Frog cast himself into the water and swam toward the dam.

Both Busy and Mrs. Beaver were working there. With lengths of tree trunks and sections of saplings and mud carried in cradled forearms, they were reinforcing and patching the dam. For a long time Cousin Frog didn't speak, knowing that Busy wouldn't like interruptions.

As he idled in the water, Maggie Magpie settled on a limb above him. "Everything that goes up must come down," she said cheerfully.

"Go up then!" Cousin Frog told her.

"Well, of all the greetings! Goodbye!" Maggie flapped away.

By and by, panting, Busy halted for breath.

"Will it hold?" Cousin Frog asked him.

"Hold it will, when we're finished."

"Good," Cousin Frog said. "I've been nervous, Busy."

"Ought to be."

"Why, if the dam won't wash out?"

Busy switched about to face him.

"I'll tell you — but don't you go spreading any alarm."

"You should know I won't."

"The dam will hold, but who can tell about water? Not even an engineer can."

"Oh?"

"Supposing the water decides to change course? Supposing it goes around the dam, right or left, and leaves the dam holding nothing?"

"I can't think it!"

"It would mean building another dam, making another pond,

and there's only my wife and me, now that the young ones took off last summer to make dams for themselves." Busy shook his head.

"And no way to prevent it, if the water takes a notion?"

"Just maybe. Likely the new course, if there is one, would be over there to the left. That's how I figure. Now see that big tree? If I could fell it just right, so's the top of it lodged tight against the end of the dam — well, maybe it would turn the water back, being a kind of small dam in itself." He shook his head again. "But it's a sight bigger tree than ever I chiseled down."

"You'll try?"

"Fool question, Cousin."

He went away, looking tired.

Swimming back to Amphibious, Cousin Frog saw that the pond was higher than ever. Just one wind-blown tatter of rush rose from the house that had been the home of the Muskrats. And now of a sudden the flood was a close roar in his ears. Surging into the pond, it began to run with a current and to pitch up waves hard to swim against.

Cousin Frog struggled to shore and, breathing hard, looked at water and sky. The sky was one solid, smothering cloud.

"Higher!" he commanded Amphibious, who waited too close to shore. "Higher yet! You'll be swept away!"

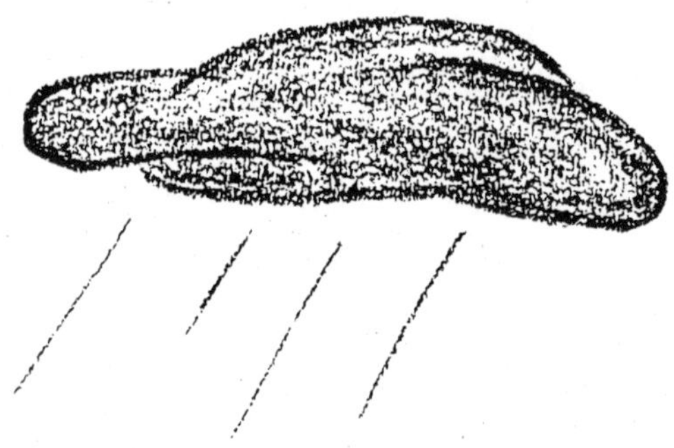

That night the rain came. It wasn't a shower but a steady gray drench that continued next day. By daylight the pond was mud-brown and unsettled and bigger than any body of water Cousin Frog ever had seen. He and Amphibious had to move up the bank again.

"Is it always like this, Cousin Frog?" Amphibious asked. "Is this the end of the world?"

"No."

"Then why is it?"

Cousin Frog felt that his worry had made him too brusque. "Look, Amphibious," he said more patiently. "It's not the rain altogether. It's the snow in the mountains, the melting snow."

"What is snow, Cousin Frog?"

The question was hard. How explain snow to one who knew

not one thing about it? Cousin Frog reflected that he didn't know much himself, since it was his practice to sleep through the winters.

"Well," he said slowly, "you might call it white rain except that it's not wet. It just falls down and lies there, and more of it comes, and it gets deep in the mountains, I've heard."

"Heard from who?"

"From whom," Cousin Frog said by way of correction. Then, "I have a friend there. Now, when the spring sun comes out, the snow runs down the mountains and pours into the streams, and so we have floods."

"Does the sun chase it down?"

"It makes it wet. That's why it runs."

"You know so much, Cousin Frog."

"All I know now is I'm cold."

Cousin Frog stretched his stiff and aching legs, one after the other. It had come on to afternoon, he guessed. He couldn't tell by the sun. Wherever he looked, it was curtained by the close, great, weeping cloud. The thought slipped into his mind that even the birds were uncomfortable now.

And so they were.

The Scissorbill Eagles had found room under a shelf of rock out of the rain, but the space was so cramped that they had to huddle and the ceiling so low that Scissorbill had to bow his proud head.

They were better off, though, than Maggie. For shelter she had only a tree. The branches above her had kept her dry at first,

but now every leaf was wet and every one dripping; and she had to
keep fluttering her wings and ruffling her feathers to avoid being
soaked to the skin. Now and then a breeze blew, as if just to
plague her, and, when it did, it seemed to her that all the stems
and leaves combined to shower her with their loads.

Better to be flying, she told herself. Better to fly and seek a
drier place. One thing for sure, unless she did so soon, she'd be too
sodden for flight. It was the rule of things, the sorry rule, she
thought, that now she should be hungry. Not hungry but
famished, weak for want of food. If only she could find one tidbit,
maybe no more than a drowned shrew in the grass! If she flew low
above the pond, in the chancy shelter of the growth along one
shore — ?

She shook herself and step by step reached the end of the limb she'd perched on and cast off, flying heavily.

After a moment she concluded it was not quite so bad as she had feared. The stroke of her wings was drying them a little despite the rain. Just beneath her, barely under water, Mousie Muskrat swam. There on the bank were Cousin Frog and Amphibious, looking miserable. She was about to call to them but remembered just in time that Cousin Frog had been rude to her at their last meeting. Still, it was comforting to see them and to see Mousie. Rain or not or flood or not, the life of the pond went on. She began to believe she'd find a bite to eat.

It was then that the accident happened.

Like a solid blow a gust of wind hit her. She faltered but

righted herself, and the gust came on stronger and tore a branch from a cluster of branches, and the branch struck her squarely and knocked her down, into the flood.

She cried out and flapped with wild wings, fanning for a hold on the air, for the hold that would lift her from the thrust and suck of the current. But her wings were no good. They only drenched her. And her legs were not meant for swimming. She felt herself being pushed along and pulled down and her body growing numb as the water made its way through her feathers. She cried out again, cried one "Please help me," knowing that no one and no thing could help.

It cannot be said that Mousie Muskrat came to the rescue, though later on he liked to think that he had. He was just swimming along under water, hoping to find safer quarters on Cousin Frog's shore than those to which the flood first had driven him. Concerned with his own business, short-sighted in the murky water, he hadn't seen Maggie. It just happened that he came to the surface hard by her.

Maggie struck out with one claw. It caught hold in the fur on his back. In what was a mere squeak she tried to shout, "Don't dive! Don't dive, Mousie!"

From the bank Cousin Frog yelled in his loudest voice, "Don't dive! Stay up! Mousie!" Then, in alarm, without thought of himself, he plunged in the water and stroked toward them. "Don't dive! Hey, stop that! Don't dive!" He saw Mousie's frightened eye. He saw that Mousie was keeping abreast of the current in spite of Maggie's wet drag. As the tide swept him by, he shouted. "Make for the shore! Make for the shore!" Looking back, he caught a glimpse of Mousie thrusting hard for the bank and knew that the two would be safe. For all his fears, Mousie was a stout swimmer.

Now, only now, did Cousin Frog think of himself. Caught in a tide that raced him along like a chip, he looked through the mists at the shores. They were too far away for a mere paddler to reach, try as he might. From such a distance that it might have been only the fret of the water against his ears, he heard the thin cry of Amphibious. "Cousin Frog! Cousin Frog!"

Stay calm, he told himself. You won't drown. Take it easy. Enjoy the ride. But the sneak voice of fear kept asking, the ride to where? To a last crash against the dam? Over the dam and far away? Around the dam to who knew what? It seemed to him that the water ran swift as the swoop of Scissorbill Eagle. It would wreck him or sweep him to lands unknown, never to come home again.

He pushed up as far as he could and saw the dam racing to meet him. Even as he looked, the angry water began to tear a new course, began to rush and froth around the end of the dam toward which the current now pointed him. There was Busy Beaver, waist-deep and head-bent, chiseling at the great tree that stood as before.

Then, with a sort of slow grace, as if in sad goodbye, its branches swept the sky, and the whole of it fell across the new torrent.

The wild water heaved against it. It pitched Cousin Frog hard

into the foliage. Then, baffled, it swung back to the main body and with it spilled over the unyielding dam.

Cousin Frog tried his legs and found them all right. His deep breaths didn't hurt him. He started feeling his way out of the foliage. When he had his head clear, he saw Busy Beaver slogging toward him through the pooled mud. "Saved," he called. "Saved."

"Not hurt?"

"No. But I was thinking of Pond Placid."

"Saved." A little lift came to Busy's tired voice. "Pond and poet together."

The Unsung Thanks
of Amphibious

The heart of Mother Earth
Keeps beating with our own,
And no one, feeling it,
Need feel himself alone.

The birds flap-soar above
And cry or sing their feat,
But each and all return
To feel the mother beat.

The sky is made to look at,
For some made to explore,
But foot to earth is homing,
And that's enough and more.

Amphibious
Sees the World

Amphibious Turtle was restless and was made all the more restless when Cousin Frog hopped to meet him. He wished he could move like that. He wished he could lift his nose above the level of the sprouting grass. The life of a young turtle was no life at all. It was just boredom, and somehow it needn't be. He must strike out for himself. He must find ways of doing and moving and seeing. Beyond the grass, across the mud, new country lay, or so it was said.

"Fine morning," Cousin Frog said. "Feel the sun."

"Fine day for you, Cousin Frog," Amphibious answered. "It's just more feet and worms for me. I want to do something."

"Everything in its time," Cousin Frog told him. "And each to its kind."

"That's what you always say. You treat me like a baby. Because you can hop, you think it's fine for me not to."

"Now, now," Cousin Frog said, knowing for a fact he did feel like a father, "Just wait a while."

"You forget how old I am. I want to do something."

"What do you want to do, little turtle?"

"Anything. Move out. See the world. Anything."

"How old do you think you are?" Cousin Frog made his voice gentle.

"Since when?"

"Since you were hatched, of course."

"I can't think back that far. Old enough to do something though."

"And how old is that?"

Amphibious thought a little. "I can't remember me at first. I bet I was around for a long time before I knew me. Couldn't that be right?"

"Days or weeks? How many? But I'll make it easy. How many times have you seen the sun come up?"

"Ten," Amphibious answered promptly.

"I've known you a good deal longer than that." Cousin Frog felt amusement soften his impatience.

"So you see, I'm older than you think."

"Why did you say 'Ten?'"

"That's as far as I can count. That's why. How old are you, Cousin Frog?"

"Maybe a hundred and seventy-five, by the risings of the sun."

"But you were young once." Amphibious's voice went plaintive. "Maybe you can't remember that."

Cousin Frog remembered. He remembered thinking, long ago, that he could swim with the best and had almost been gobbled by a trout. It was the way of life, he thought, the way of the young, to go forth too soon. And where could little Amphibious go, anyhow? What could he do? Turtles, young and old, were condemned to dull lives. He said gently, "I want you to learn, Amphibious."

"How can I, though? How can I when you won't let me? Just answer that."

"Don't be cross," Cousin Frog said. "It's not like you. You see, I don't want you to be hurt."

"Don't worry."

"All right, Amphibious. Just what's on your mind?"

"I said anything. Anything but this. I don't know a bit more than mud and worms and the inside of my shell. Other people hop and run and climb and fly. I wish I could fly, that's what I wish. I want to see the world. Please, Cousin Frog, let me do it and help me."

For a long time Cousin Frog was silent. He felt the strings of an idea, a frightening idea, and was almost sorry it had entered his mind. He said, "I wouldn't want you to get discouraged and crawl into hiding and never see the world at all."

"I'll try," Amphibious told him, too eagerly. "Whatever you suggest, I'll try, and I promise not to be discouraged."

"Even if it scares you? Even though it might be dangerous?"

"Even if it scares me," Amphibious repeated. "Even though it might be dangerous."

"Be patient, then. Don't be cranky. I'll see."

Cousin Frog swam across Pond Placid, his idea growing as he swam. In back of him he heard Amphibious Turtle's frail cry, "I'm sorry, Cousin Frog. Cousin Frog, I love you." He said, "Good morning," to Busy Beaver, who had risen early and was chipping through a small aspen tree. Busy Beaver stopped long enough to squint at the sky. The morning sun was in his eyes. "Fair," he answered after spitting out a mouthful of wood. Then he bent back to his task.

Cousin Frog floated idly in the water, his big eyes fixed on the worker, but, though his body was idle, his brain was not. It took some doing to talk Busy Beaver into anything. At last he said, "I hate to bother a working man."

Busy Beaver spit again. "Speaks well for you."

"Would you be interested in a project?"

"Project?" asked Busy Beaver through his teeth.

"A piece of work, that is? A little chore?"

Ever since he found he could make words rhyme, Busy had been rhyming them. He gave some thought to his answer without halting the snick-snack of cutting the tree. Then he recited his lines:

Busy's my name, and work is my lot
But not pieces of work. So, Cousin, I'm not.

Cousin Frog put a thoughtful hand to his jaw. He spoke as if talking to himself. "I should have known better. You probably can't do it anyway."

Busy Beaver jerked upright, braced by his tail. His voice was sharp. "I meant shan't, not can't."

Cousin Frog said, "Huh," and started to swim away. He hadn't swum far until Busy called after him, "Hold the boat, you old croak throat."

Cousin Frog paddled back. "I was thinking," he said, "of a teeter-totter."

"And you think I can't make one?" Busy Beaver laughed. "Nothing to it. Cut a cross log and drop a longer tree over it."

"I would want the long end of the totter – or is it teeter? – to dip into the water."

"Uh-huh," said Busy, and again a little rhyme came to his lips.

> *It is no matter, teeter or totter.*
> *The long end touches the water.*

Cousin Frog went on. "I should like it to be near a tree."

"I would know better how to do it if I knew what you aim to do?" Busy Beaver said as a question.

"You believe in education, don't you?"

"Engineers do."

"It's something I'm thinking up for Amphibious," Cousin Frog said, not wanting to explain his plan too far in advance. Later would be better, he felt, after he had put all the pieces together and made surer, within himself, that the plan wasn't crazy.

"Amphibious has to learn."

"Learn what? Teeter and totter?"

"The world," Cousin Frog answered. "But never mind right now. It's not time."

Before more questions could be asked, Cousin Frog left.

* * *

Now began days and nights of patient waiting. Cousin Frog watched the sun come up and make its journey across the sky and go to rest in the western mountains. When the dark settled, he floated in the water silently, keeping in his throat the night song that wanted to be sung.

At times, thinking he heard movement in the bushes on the far shore, he would call across the pond, "Ursa. Ursa Minor." As if in answer G. H. Owl would hoot, far off, "Who? Who?," and Cousin Frog would hope that Molly Cottontail was safe, for Owl was a night hunter and against Pond Placid rules, obeyed by all the rest, last year had hunted the banks and grassy opens there. But it wasn't for G. H. Owl that Cousin Frog listened. It was for a sound heard often before but not heard now by night or day.

The serviceberries ripened, and those withered that the birds had not enjoyed, and the chokecherries came on, green at first, then red as fairy paint, waiting for the frost that would turn their red to purple. The aspen trees looked tired and dropped the first leaves of their loads, and the nights grew shorter, and now and then chill touched the evening air.

24

And Cousin Frog waited and listened.

He worried Amphibious Turtle. "You act so funny," Amphibious told him. "Just floating and looking. Please, what ails you, Cousin?"

"Patience," Cousin Frog answered. "Patience."

"Is that part of my education?" Amphibious asked meekly.

"It's only to pushy people that patience gives a pain."

Amphibious sighed. "It doesn't seem much like seeing the world."

"He'll come," Cousin Frog said almost to himself. "He always comes."

Amphibious didn't know what was meant, nor would Cousin Frog say any more. Instead, as dusk settled over the pond, he slipped back in the water.

The dark closed in, but by and by the moon came up, orange at first, then silver as bullberry leaves in the sun, and shadows moved along the shore lines, and the pond shone like a mirror seen by candlelight.

And then Cousin Frog heard without mistake. There was a thrashing of the bushes on the western bank, as if something big pushed its way through without thought of fear.

Cousin Frog cried out, "Ursa! Ursa Minor!", and paddled ahead as fast as he could.

Over the water rolled a rough but good-natured voice. "How your own se'f?"

Cousin Frog swam even faster and presently pulled up to the bank.

Before him stood Ursa, Ursa Minor, the friendly brown bear from the mountains, looking big as a horse against the moon-lighted skyline.

They didn't say much at first. Westerners seldom do when they meet after being long apart. So for some time Cousin Frog just kept gazing, and Ursa wore a big smile.

At last Cousin Frog said, "Late." After a pause he added, "I wondered."

"It was almighty fair in the mountains," Ursa answered. "This here old cub follered his snoot to a dude ranch, and the garbage was some, it was that. Them dudes dump out a galore of fat fixin's, they do now. From what they leave, an idjit would wonder what they et, them dudes."

"They treated you all right?"

"They shined, that's what! They sp'iled me, passin' out cookies and sweets and watermelon. They allowed this cub was a plumb ornament to the country. Reminds me. Chokecherries ripe? That's what I come for, and to see my old pardners."

"Close to ripe," Cousin Frog answered.

After another silence Ursa more or less asked — for in the

mountains more or less asking was politer than asking — "Never knowed you before to have the wide-eye over my comin'?"

"No," Cousin Frog told him. "I wanted to beg a small favor."

"Just tell me, Cousin, and I'll see she's done, that I will. But will it be fun?"

"Educational," Cousin Frog said, and as he swam away he called back, "I want Busy Beaver on hand. Tell you all about it before daybreak."

* * *

For several reasons Cousin Frog had wanted some privacy in what he had to admit was an experiment. The presence of a crowd might make Amphibious nervous and so less able to play his part. If the plan failed, if it just fizzled out, not many would laugh, but Scissorbill certainly would; and while older folk could stand up to snickers and slurs, a young one could be hurt and discouraged. Maybe Amphibious would turn his back on education forever. And by their very presence crowds worked against a calm try-out.

But, as Cousin Frog feared, all Pond Placid woke up early next morning. Only a few knew what would take place that day, but everyone was expectant. Maggie Magpie didn't know herself but still had routed Pond Placid from sleep by crying, "Get up! Something up! Something up! Up and see!" Why, she asked, as she fluttered around, were Busy Beaver and Cousin Frog so tight-lipped? What had they been planning when they met beyond earshot of anyone? And here was Ursa, arrived just last night, who had few words for his old friends?

28

From all sections they gathered around what promised to be the scene of activity. Even the Muskrats had ventured down to the main pond. Mollie Cottontail was there, and the Chipmunks, and Mephitis and his wife and, of course, Maggie. No one had expected Needles the Porcupine, who ordinarily drowsed during the daylight hours, but here he was, if only half-awake. Scissorbill Eagle, seeing the activity from far in the sky, had come down with a rush of kingly wings and settled in a tree. Amphibious, as ignorant as the rest of what was in store, floated out in the pond, feeling small and out of place.

The air sounded to chirps and churrings and squealings and grunts and guesses and conversations, and all added to a waiting excitement.

Before many were awake, Cousin Frog had gone over the plans with Busy Beaver and Ursa, and now Busy was busy making the teeter-totter while Cousin Frog watched closely and Ursa looked on.

From his perch Scissorbill rasped out, "What's going on here?"

Ursa gazed up and laughed at the King of Birds. He answered,
"A heap, pardner, a heap, that's what. If'n you had more head and
less beak, maybe you would savvy, just maybe you would."

Scissorbill drew himself up. "I am the King of Birds."

Again Ursa laughed. "This here cub thinks there ought to be
a revolution. You speak pore for them with wings, you do now.
Savin' the bats, o'course. All bats is batty."

For the moment Busy Beaver had tired of his gnawing, and,
besides, some lines were running in his head. He turned his eyes up

to Scissorbill.

> *All bats are batty,*
> *As all gnats are gnatty,*
> *And all can take wing;*
> *But they haven't beaks*
> *From which wisdom leaks,*
> *Provided there's some in the king.*

Ursa looked at Busy Beaver with admiration. "You shine, old chisel tooth," he said. "You're some now, you are, or else eagles got brains, which they ain't. Dock off wings and beak, and what have you got? A feather with a flutter, that's what."

Encouraged by the words, Busy went back to work. Presently, as the chatter of the onlookers grew, a tree fell, the tree that was to be the crosspiece of the teeter-totter. It lay just where Busy had wanted it to lie, lengthwise of the pond and close to shore.

Now Busy Beaver went to Cousin Frog. "After I fell it, Ursa and I can roll the teeter or totter along the crosspiece so's the short end will be close to the tree here." The tree was big. High above them, a heavy branch thrust out from it.

Cousin Frog nodded. Now, seeing Amphibious looking forlorn and deserted, he stroked over to him. "It won't be long," he said.

Amphibious answered in a small voice. "For what?"

"That's why I haven't told you, so you won't be flustered

beforehand."

"Is knowing worse than not knowing?" Amphibious asked, still in a small voice. "I'd like to pull myself in my shell, Cousin Frog."

Cousin Frog spoke with a confidence he didn't feel entirely. "You're going to take a trip, Amphibious. You're going to see the world. Don't get scared. There's no danger."

Amphibious was silent until across the water he heard Ursa speaking his peculiar language. He asked, trying to forget whatever it was that was going to happen to him, "What makes him talk that way, Cousin Frog?"

"He's a friend, a good friend. Never forget that."

"But what makes him talk that way?"

"The mountains," Cousin Frog answered.

"I guess I see."

Cousin Frog tried to be stern. "Don't you begin speaking as he does."

"That I won't. I won't that," Amphibious replied, and, suddenly realizing he almost had, he drew his head into his shell in embarrassment.

There came a great crackling of wood and the whoosh of a falling tree and a hard splash in the water. Then came high riffles that rocked and half-blinded them, but they could see that the totter was down, at right angles over the crosspiece. The branches and leaves of the fallen tree dipped in the water.

Ursa and Busy Beaver now started rolling the downed tree to its place under the big limb of the tree left standing. Busy sang as he pushed.

There's nothing like an engineer
And all his special gear
To drop a tree or build a dam.
An engineer I am.
I dam and cut and cut and dam,
And water stops and trees go slam,
If engineers are near.

When Busy Beaver and Ursa had got the log to its place, they signaled to Cousin Frog. He swam toward them for a final size-up. To Busy Beaver he said, "Thanks. Your part is done." He turned to Ursa. "Sure you have it fixed in your head, now?"

"This here brain is bustin' with it," Ursa answered. "Ole hoss, you don't have to write it on a sharp stick and stab me ear to ear to get an idee in my skull. Just sound off, military-like, when it pleases your cousinship."

With that, Ursa started climbing the standing tree.

Cousin Frog nodded his satisfaction and went to Amphibious. "Come," he said.

Together they swam to the tangle of leaves and branches that dipped in the water, to the long end of the totter, that is. "Now, Amphibious," Cousin Frog advised, "I want you to hold to every twig and branch that you can. Clamp on to them. Hold with your front feet. Hold with your back. Hold with your mouth. Hold tight with them all."

Amphibious wanted to ask why, but he began to do as he was told, though his eyes kept going to Cousin Frog. He got a hold on a twig with one front foot, then on another with the other. As best he could, he clutched with his hind feet. Last of all, he stretched his neck and got a bite on a twig overhead.

Cousin Frog half-circled about him, making sure. "Ready?" he asked. Amphibious couldn't answer with the twig clenched in his mouth. He tried to nod his head instead, and then he closed his eyes.

Silence fell on the spectators.

Cousin Frog backed away in order to have a full view. Ursa had moved out on the big limb. He waved an all right.

Of a sudden Cousin Frog felt fear in him, seeing Amphibious spread-eagled and helpless in the tree's foliage. If things didn't go right? If he was wrong? And Amphibious was so young and so small — and so trusting! But things carried to a certain point had to be carried on. You couldn't turn back, for reasons so mixed that they had to be sorted out later.

Cousin Frog lifted his head and sang out his orders, in tones not too steady.

> *One for the high ride.*
> *Two for the low.*
> *Three to get ready,*
> *And four to LET GO!*

Then everything seemed to happen at once. With a wild mountain yell Ursa dropped from the limb to the totter, hitting

the end of it with a bump that drove it down toward the ground. The branched end of the tree whipped from the water and leaped high to the sound of torn air. For a second or less the watchers saw Amphibious holding on desperately. Then the branches whipped to a stop and snapped him loose. He shot in the air, high and higher. "Like a somersaultin' bird," Ursa thought while he stared, for as he rose Amphibious was spinning head over heels and heels over head. Anxiousness brought a croak to Cousin Frog's throat.

In the craning silence the scared voice of Amphibious reached down, now weak and then strong as the spin aimed his head at heaven or earth. "Holy smokes. HOLY SMOKES!"

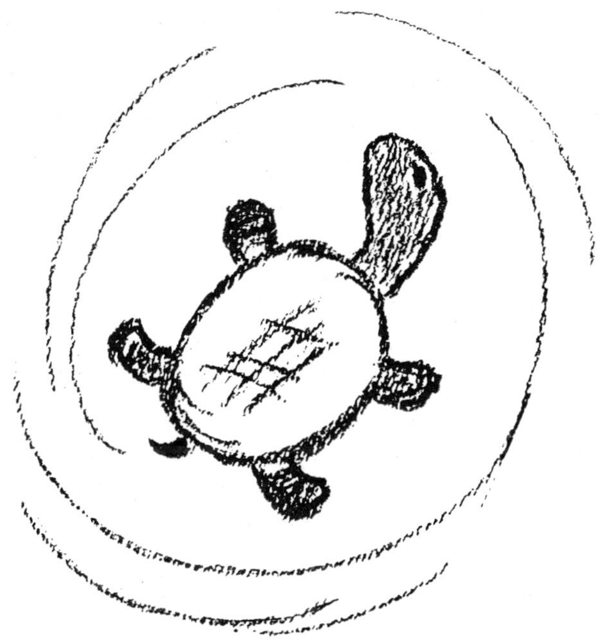

Amphibious shot to the top of his climb and, still spinning, plunged down. He landed with a great splash, considering his size.

With all the power of his muscles Cousin Frog hastened to Amphibious. "All right? All right, boy?" he panted, not just because of the exercise.

Amphibious answered in almost a whisper. "Please take me to shore, Cousin Frog. I spin when I swim."

On the far bank, after an unsteady trip up the slope, he spoke again. "I wish you had told me, Cousin Frog. Up there the world spins."

"No. You spun. The earth doesn't turn."

"I was there, Cousin Frog." He had too much respect for Cousin Frog to say that Cousin Frog wasn't. "The sky would be on the ground and the ground in the sky, and then they'd swap, Cousin Frog. It scared me bad."

The day had been too much, the day had and the fright and the world turning. Of a sudden Amphibious began crying. He put his hands to his eyes in shame. "I'm sorry," he said. "I'm so shook."

Out of habit Cousin Frog answered, "Shaken." Then he felt ashamed of himself. Now was no time for lessons in grammar. He said gently, "Now. Now. It's all over. You did just fine. Dry your tears."

Amphibious couldn't, for a long time.

At last Cousin Frog thought up a lullaby and sang it over and over in his softest frog's voice, and Amphibious closed his eyes and finally smiled a little smile. "It's a big place. Thank you, Cousin Frog," he said and fell into a fidgety sleep.

Cousin Frog stayed by his side, singing again when Amphibious stirred. As he sang, he heard like a rumbling echo the now-and-then "Who?" of G. H. Owl. His lullaby went:

Sleep, little turtle.
No cause to cry.
Folks saw you hurtle,
Brave in the sky.

So rest and so sleep.
You did your part well,
And your deed will keep
Like an ever-heard bell,

Like a bell glorious,
Hailing the valorous.
Hurrah for Amphibious.
Sleep.   Sleep.

Meters for Mollie

Oh, Mollie with the melting eyes,
Are you prudent, are you wise,
Dining when the day is spent
And G. H. Owl is plunder-bent?

Not all your beauty will suffice
To turn that night-time prowler nice,
Nor depth of eye nor feel of fur
Deter his savage beak and spur.

It would be better if you dined
At hours when G. H. Owl is blind.
Please never let that greedy sinner
Devour your beauty for his dinner.

Now we will help, if help we can,
And Cousin Frog has planned a plan
To use because your stomach's rhyme
Seems not set up for daylight time.

G. H. Owl

Mollie Cottontail ran through the bushes, careful to keep under their cover. The night was black, without even a star showing, and she had to run blind, bumping into the undergrowth and tripping and falling. Halted, she would rest for an instant and suck for breath and feel of her side and run again, her paw wet with blood from her wound.

Back of her in the night, or overhead or ahead of her, somewhere for sure, were a great beak and hooked talons and eyes that saw in the dark.

She cried, "Cousin Frog! Cousin Frog!" and cowered down, her blood pounding, for the black death could hear.

The pond shimmered and lost itself in the night, like something that crossed the eye and was gone. It seemed asleep or empty or both, desolate as a grave. Nothing moved. Nobody spoke. There were just herself and her wound and her wild heart and the dark, and the unseen death that could see. "Cousin Frog! Cousin Frog!"

"This way, Mollie. This way."

She ran to him and cowered under a small growth of rushes. His body was a blob, cut in half by the dark water he half-rested in.

Her news burst out of her. "He's after me. My side!" She turned so he could see it. "G. H. Owl. He hunts Pond Placid again."

As if in proof, the hunting cry of the great horned owl, like the voice of a lost ghost, troubled the air. "Who — who — who-who-who — who."

"Deeper in the bushes." Cousin Frog's tone pushed her back. "Last year, your man. Now you." His gaze went to her wound. "How bad?"

"A slash. I rolled under a rose bush."

"What's this shindig about, I'm askin'?" It was Ursa Minor, who for all his bulk and boldness had approached as quietly as a cat.

"G. H. Owl hunts Mollie."

Ursa's words came out of a gust. "Hunts Mollie! Ahh! Wish I had wings. This child would larn him. Owl? Ain't no killin' machine got any right to fly, I'm thinkin'."

"He does, though," Mollie said. There was a shake in her voice.

"What now, Tadpole?"

Cousin Frog did not take offense, for none was intended. He said to Mollie, "Change mealtimes. Eat in daylight. He can't see well then."

"There is a way of things," she answered. "You sing at dawn and dusk."

Cousin Frog had no answer; but wouldn't he feel a fool, singing at high noon? Besides, he had no voice then. He said to Mollie, "Go away. Keep under the bushes. Go hungry, but keep under the bushes."

After she had gone, Ursa said, "One killer kills the peace. One G. H. Owl."

"And man, when he comes," Cousin Frog reminded him, and Ursa answered, "Man," and thought a minute and added, "On'y they was good to me at the dude ranch."

"Because they couldn't shoot. Closed season."

"Yeah. Closed season."

"But about Mollie?"

"Why don't we call on Mister Owl?" Ursa asked. "All of us?"

Cousin Frog answered, "Hmm. To tell him what?"

"Tell him what's what, that's what. And that there Scissorbill, callin' hisself the King of Birds, he could do something maybe."

"Hmm," Cousin Frog repeated. "It can't hurt, I guess."

The next morning he gave Maggie Magpie her instructions, and she took wing noisily, crying, "Assemble, one and all. Hear ye, assemble." Now that she had a real message, she was all business and all voice.

They gathered, all of them, about the bank where Cousin Frog sat. Amphibious Turtle, not knowing what the meeting was about, told Cousin Frog brightly, "I haven't seen so many together since I took my trip."

Cousin Frog hushed him. He announced, "G. H. Owl hunts the pond again. Show them, Mollie."

A frightened murmur rose among them, among the Chipmunks and the Muskrats and the Skunks, all of whom had reason to know about G. H. Owl; and Maggie, usually so talkative, snapped "Owl," remembering a night last year when a shadow had seized her fledgling.

"I heard him – like something in my sleep," Memphitis Skunk said.

"A dream, I told myself it was," Tommy Chipmunk put in.

From Maggie Magpie came, "I had my head under my wing."

Even those who had heard Owl last night, Cousin Frog thought, hadn't wanted to face up to the truth. "Ursa wants us to call on him," he said into the little clamor.

"And tell him what's what."

Cousin Frog asked, "And then?"

"And then —" Ursa rubbed his jaw. "Why," he said as he looked around, "for an enforcer we got the King of Birds."

Perched on a limb above him, Scissorbill lifted a leg and scratched his side uneasily. "I'm night-blind," he said.

Ursa let out a great snort. "Some king! King under the sun, mouse under the moon!" He turned to the rest. "Let's talk to Owl, anyhow. What say, Cousin Frog?"

They set out, everyone of them, for the old dead cottonwood north of the pond where Owl chose to sleep. For some it was a long journey, and hot, for the sun shone bright and there was not a whisper of breeze.

G. H. Owl sat asleep on a limb. Or maybe he wasn't asleep. You never could tell. They came to a halt underneath and around him, not too close.

"Owl," Cousin Frog called. "G. H. Owl."

The eyes opened then, the great, wide, murderous eyes, and the brutal beak went to snapping like the chop of teeth. "Who's disturbing my sleep?"

Cousin Frog answered, "I am. Cousin Frog. In behalf of the pond."

"Behalf and be done." Owl's voice was like the chafing of limbs in a wind.

"We want peace at Pond Placid. You're outlawed."

G. H. Owl blinked his eyes. "That'll take some doing. Just

who's going to run me off."

Ursa reared on his hind legs and roared up at him, "Git in distance, butcher bird!"

Cousin Frog's eyes went to Scissorbill. Scissorbill would not meet them.

Owl kept snapping his beak. You might have thought the sound it made was dry laughter, though the beak could bite through bones.

"Be wise," Cousin Frog told him.

"I got a reputation for wisdom." In the glare of the sun he peered around. "That cottontail with you?"

Mollie shrank behind Busy Beaver.

"You'll not get her."

"One rabbit dinner, one gone owl?"

Mousie Muskrat quavered, "If we could be sure, then. . ."

Ursa drowned him out. "No deals," he growled. "None whatsoever."

"But," — Mousie's words came almost in a whisper — "you're big, and we're. . ."

"No deals," Cousin Frog said. He spoke to Ursa, "I told you

it was no use. Let's go." His friends looked at him with disappointment. He knew they had expected more.

As they started away, the dry laughter followed them, and further along they heard Owl's, "Good luck."

They talked again, back at the pond, making a jabber that Cousin Frog cut off. "We are too many," he said.

"Too many and too noisy, that's what we be," Ursa put in, feeling sure he knew what Cousin Frog had in mind. "Name a boss committee, Tadpole."

Seeing the others nod, Cousin Frog said, "All right. I name Ursa, Busy Beaver, Mollie and Maggie."

"And me?" Amphibious asked meekly.

"Yes. Sure. And you."

Ursa said to Cousin Frog, for the benefit of the rest, "You'll be the chief, ne'en to say. We'll be froze for sure without one brain in the outfit."

Again the company nodded.

"We'll do best alone," Cousin Frog told them. "Please don't act curious, no matter what."

One by one they wandered off, until only Cousin Frog, Ursa, Mollie, Maggie and Amphibious remained.

The committee members appeared pretty solemn, Busy Beaver thought. For himself, he wasn't so downcast. He even thought up a few lines:

That wise old Owl has slipped a cog
To match his wits with Cousin Frog.
I'll bet a sapling on the fight
And pay off two if I'm not right.

Ursa asked of Cousin Frog, "Any idees?"

"One," Cousin Frog said. "By dawn and by dark you stay with Mollie."

"Yes, Ma'am," Ursa told Mollie, trying to still her fears with light talk. "Pleased to keep you company."

He turned to Cousin Frog and waited, seeing him close-mouthed and wide-eyed, lost in thoughts of his own.

At last Ursa said, "We taken the hint," and motioned Busy, Amphibious, Maggie and Mollie away and then, with a last look at Cousin Frog, followed after Mollie.

On the lip of the water Cousin Frog sat as if dead, only his wide eyes showing he wasn't. He sat there all afternoon and into the dark, after a while hearing the night pulse to G. H. Owl's call. "Who-who — who-who-who — who-who." Ursa and Mollie would be listening, he knew. Ursa and Mollie. It was then that the big idea came to him, as he knew it would if he bothered his mind long enough. Not until it came did he go to sleep.

The committee met again the next morning. Everyone looked at Cousin Frog, hardly daring to hope he had come up with an answer so soon. He told them, "We need a digger."

They didn't understand. He added, "An earth-mover."

Ursa examined his paws, "I can dig some," he said.

"I wasn't thinking of you, not of any of you."

"Who, then?"

"Blow Nose Badger."

The answer astonished them.

"Blow Nose!" Ursa exclaimed. "He ain't rightly one of us, that he ain't."

Busy Beaver said, "Whew! Body and mind, he stinks."

"He's our digger." Cousin Frog raised his eyes to the branch above him. "Maggie, tell him to come."

"He won't."

Ursa made a noise in his throat. "Oh, yes, he will, I'm thinkin', else my daddy was a bird." He cocked an eye at Maggie. "Lead on, rememberin' that fur don't fly."

The sun stood straight overhead before they returned, bringing Blow Nose with them. He was about the size of Busy Beaver, and he tried to hang back, his hair on end, only to move when Ursa, who followed him, slapped him on the rump.

"What's the idea?" Blow Nose asked Cousin Frog. His voice sounded strangled.

"Got a job for you," Cousin Frog answered.

Bow Nose retreated a step, and his nostrils wrinkled between the white lines of his snoot and blew out an evil spray. Ursa raised a paw as if to cuff him again. " 'Pears by now you'd know stink don't get you nowheres. Say yes afore I get my dander up."

Cousin Frog said mildly, "For the best digger in the whole country, it's not much of a job."

"I got my own digging to do." Blow Nose lifted a paw and looked at it. "Blunt already."

"Blunt?" It was Ursa who spoke. "Them claws are like a passel of knives. You can dig fast as a horse can walk, that's what this child hears."

Blow Nose wheeled about to face Ursa. "If I was your size!"

"Easy, old pardner. You ain't."

Cousin Frog asked, "Mollie, where do you usually eat?"

"Across the pond. In the glade." She felt of the healing wound in her side. "That's where I got this."

"To the other side, then." Cousin Frog took to the water, followed by Busy Beaver and Amphibious. Maggie flew on over. Ursa, Mollie and Blow Nose went around by the dam. Presently they all met in the glade, which was closed in by willows and black birch and a few old cottonwoods. The grass there made a soft carpet.

Cousin Frog said, "Maggie, whatever you see, for once keep your mouth shut."

"You forget I have reason to." Maggie closed her beak with a click.

To Ursa Cousin Frog said, "You'll need patience."

"Mostly, this here old bear ain't long on it, but hunkydory."

"And, Mollie, you'll have to be brave, braver than you've ever been."

She nodded, trembling a little.

"Ursa, I want you to lie down on your stomach, flat as you can. Extend your legs, all four of them."

"Orders from an idjit," Ursa answered good-naturedly and did as he was told.

"Now, Blow Nose, make some marks. I want a hole dug that will fit him, so when he lies down again, he'll be level with the ground."

"Now what in the name of — "

"You like G. H. Owl?"

"Like Owl! Sure. Much as I like a steel trap."

"Then do as I tell you."

"Should've given me a hint before."

Blow Nose went around Ursa, making little scratches in the

earth to outline his body. When Ursa got up, Blow Nose began to dig with good will. Anyone else would have made slow work of it. Not Blow Nose. The sod and dirt flew at the hard, deep, powerful scratches of his claws. They fitted Ursa into the hole once for size, finding they had to make it a little deeper for the bulge in his stomach. Then it was just right. When he settled himself into it, the whole top of him was flush with the ground.

Cousin Frog said, "We'll need the loose dirt to tuck in around him. Busy Beaver, can you carry those pieces of sod into the trees, out of sight?"

Sure thing." He went to work at once, cradling the sod in his arms and ambling off into the trees. By the time he had finished, the sun had closed half its eye behind the skyline. G. H. Owl would be getting his sight soon.

Busy Beaver filled in the cracks and smoothed out the dirt around Ursa. Even in daylight, you hardly would have known Ursa was there.

"Don't move now. Lie quiet," Cousin Frog told him. "Now, Mollie pretend to feed just in front of Ursa. Stay within reach."

A light broke on Ursa. "Tadpole," he said through the dirt around his nose, "you shine. Now don't you worry none, Mollie."

"Patience," Cousin Frog said. "Courage." As if it had just occurred to him, he added for Ursa's benefit, "Don't let him see you, not any time."

He led the others away.

* * *

To Ursa it seemed like forever, lying on his stomach in the damp, half-stifling ground. He wanted to change positions. It didn't come natural to a bear, lying flat and spread-eagled. He wanted to scratch himself. Must have picked up a wood tick some place. But he lay quiet, with one eye fixed on Mollie, who was making as if to eat, though she trembled in every fiber.

Then the cry came, that long-quick-long cry of the owl thinking of his kill. Perched in a tree some place, about to take silent wing, he might be asking himself where best to hunt. "It was "Where?" he was asking, not "Who?" "Where — where — where-where-where — where — where." Ursa saw Mollie stiffen and get hold of herself and go back to nosing at the grass.

And it seemed to him of a sudden that he had waited too long. He heard close above him the hard whosh of wings lowered

as brakes. He saw the great legs, almost in his eye, and the savage
talons extended. He struck out with one paw, struck out with
quick might, and feathers flew, and a furious shriek knifed

through the night. He could make out all of Owl now, knocked
from his balance, knocked from his target, fanning his big wings
and barely climbing again. Ursa flattened back in his hole so as not
to be seen, pausing just long enough to make sure about Mollie. He
heard a thump in the woods and guessed that Owl had hit a tree,
but the hard wing-beats sounded again, and he knew that Owl
somehow had kept on.

When he pulled in his paw, he saw half of Owl's tail caught in
it. It would, he thought, be hard to fly with only half a tail.

* * *

Morning came, a dark and cloudy morning. Ursa had made his report the night before, and now the committee was wondering. Had G. H. Owl left for good? Had he left at all? Did he know he'd been tricked, and, knowing, would he stay on?

Ursa was positive. "No, indeedy, he caught nary sight of me, before, durin' or atterwards. For all he knows the ground came up and catched his tail."

"Maggie, take a scout, will you?" Cousin Frog asked.

She came back shortly, so excited that she had trouble getting words out. "He's leaving!" She reported after cawing her throat clear. "He's going to leave."

"No?" Cousin Frog sat back, feeling his body ease and expand. "Really? When?"

"This very day, he says."

"In daylight?"

Maggie peered up at the low and sunless sky. "Dark enough, he says."

Ursa was jumping up and down, his fur moving to the jiggle of his fat. "Poor doin's not to tell him goodbye. Wouldn't be fittin'. Come one, come all. Come on!" His voice carried to the farthest reaches of the pond.

He led the way, followed by the committee, and on their trail gathered all of Pond Placid, including even that half-outsider, Blow Nose Badger.

G. H. Owl sat as before, except that on close view he showed but half a tail. There was no laughter now in the snapping of his beak.

"Leaving, huh?" Cousin Frog said to him. "Glad you thought better of it."

"Worse of it," G. H. Owl rasped. "It's agin nature."

"What?"

"Some dirty black magic, that's what." He snapped his beak bitterly. Mixes up the mind. Can't tell what?"

They all waited.

"It's agin nature, I say, agin nature when a rabbit up and tears your tail out."

With that, G. H. Owl cast off from the limb, flying

uncertainly, and presently was out of sight.

Then Cousin Frog and Ursa, assisted by Blow Nose Badger, told the story to the people of Pond Placid, and they all laughed in their ways. They chirped and squeaked and churred, and Mephitis Skunk rolled over and over.

As they set out for home the sun came out, and the crowd lazed along, happy to be rid of G. H. Owl, still laughing because Owl thought Mollie had torn off half his tail. Going along, Cousin Frog thought up a song, honoring Ursa. Because it was in Ursa's honor, he used the words that Ursa would have.

After a little while all were singing it and all moved to its rhythm. At the last line of each stanza they halted and tramped their feet, one, two, three, four, or, in the case of Maggie, hovered overhead and flapped wings to the time. Only Scissorbill had no heart for such foolishness.

Here is the song they sang:

> *G. H. Owl is leavin',*
> *G. H. Owl is leavin',*
> *And nary one is grievin',*
> *No, nary one is grievin'.*
> *Mark time, three, four!*
>
> *G. H. Owl is leavin'.*
> *So long to his thievin'*
> *Of lives that us'ns believe in.*
> *Nary one is grievin',*
> *Take that fer shore!*
>
> *Ursa and the Cottontail*
> *Set a smart trap in the dale.*
> *Without a tail Owl can not sail.*
> *To them two, then, we holler hail.*
> *Good luck galore!*

It had been quite a time, they agreed before they scattered, even if Scissorbill didn't think so. And now there was not an enemy, not in Nature, which had turned kind, and not in water or on land. Or so they thought.

The Song of the Hounds

Hard on our padprints, our Man Master, run,
Eye sharp for Ursa, hand quick on your gun!
Bay, hounds, bay!
Blue Tick and Red Bone, now hold to the scent.
Soon we will catch him, now soon he'll be spent.
Bay away!
Keen in our noses the smell of his flight.
Hot in the grasses the heat of his fright.
Run, dogs, run!
What were we born for if not to give chase?
Lungs for the long run and legs for the race?
Fun, hounds, fun!
When he pants to a stop, then run in and dodge free,
Bitten and badgered, he'll look for a tree.
Howl, hounds, bay!
Master will come then and fill him with lead.
Ho for a frolic, friends, over the dead!

Ursa Asks Help

Ursa Minor lay flat behind a fallen tree, his head raised just enough for one eye to see over and beyond it. Except for the light, noiseless breaths he allowed himself, which stirred his big chest hardly at all, he did not move. Within easy earshot a man walked, and the man had a gun.

The man stepped slowly, talking to himself, his eyes turned down to the earth save now and then for a quick look around. He was backtracking, Ursa knew, going back along the padprints he had followed before. He stopped now and stooped and squinted and with a finger outlined a footmark Ursa had left in the rain-softened ground, as if to prove to himself he had been on the trail of a bear sure enough.

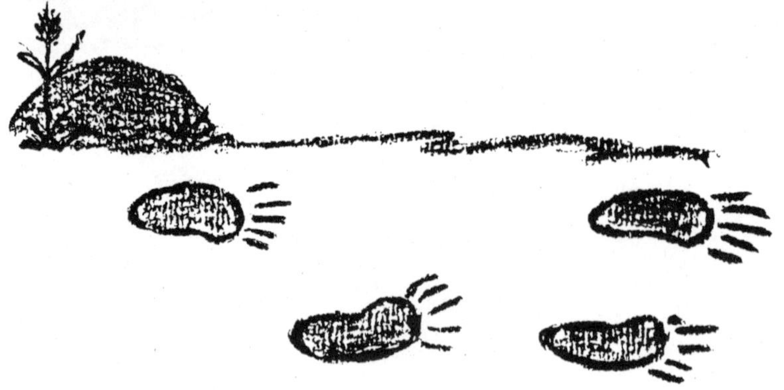

Earlier Ursa had seen the hunter before the hunter had seen him and had run along an old trail, careless of the pad-and-claw track he left, and, once surely beyond sight, had dodged toward the pond, slipped into the water just above the dam and swum quietly upstream, hugging the bank so as to be screened by the growth on shore. When he came to a gravel bar, he drew himself up and went on. Prints would hardly show there, and the water he dripped soon would dry up. Then he started following the man who was following him.

At the edge of the pond, where Ursa had taken to the water, the man stopped and scratched his head. The gun he had held up to readiness he let hang in his hand. After a while he turned, his shoulders slack, and began retracing his steps. Ursa went flat behind the log, knowing the down-turned eyes hadn't seen him.

Now, watching, with the scent of the man strong in his nose and the voice of the man plain to his ears, Ursa felt alert but not frightened. Man? Man. His nose was weak and his hearing poor, and his eyes didn't see what wild eyes would see. Without his gun he was next door to nothing.

He wasn't afraid of anyone, Ursa told himself as the man straightened and began to walk on, shaking his head. Not anyone, winged, four-footed or two-footed. It was a good way to feel. Then, suddenly, hearing the man speak to himself in a gust of words, Ursa knew fear, not fear of anyone but fear of anyones, of someones, fear of what he knew he could not defeat.

When the man was gone from sight, he rose slowly, went to the dam and shambled across and started up the shore. The pond lay peaceful, and the peaceful sky lay in it, like a promise to all; and for a moment Ursa thought that maybe water and heaven were treating him, were being as nice as they could for this, his last sight of Pond Placid.

"Hi, Cub." It was Cousin Frog, planted on the bank as usual. By his side little Amphibious lay asleep.

Ursa didn't answer. He sat down and stared across the water. With the sun low in the west, the trees on the far shore, mirrored in the pond, reached towards them, as real almost as the trees themselves. It was the hour of no wind, Ursa thought, the time of no fret.

At last he said, "Reckon this old bear will take off for the mountains tonight."

Cousin Frog considered. Then, as if he understood, he answered, "I saw him."

"Aw! Man!"

"What, then?"

"Him alone don't figger. I could rub him out if killin' came natural to me."

Cousin Frog waited, thinking it better for Ursa to go on as he chose.

"He talked to hisself, the man did. I got so I savvy a little of that man jabber."

Now Cousin Frog prompted him. "So what did he say?"

"I don't need no help, Tadpole. It ain't becomin' to ask." Ursa's little grunt didn't sound funny. "Me, the biggest critter around!"

"Ask," Cousin Frog said, his voice sharp.

"Oh, I guess I wouldn't be plumb shamed to ask, Tadpole. But where's the body kin help me?"

"When?"

"When the man comes with his hounds."

"Hounds? Bat them back home."

"Nope. Nope. You don't understand." Ursa sighed, and the sigh seemed to riffle the now-darkening water. "I ain't up to it, I ain't. They got noses. They's fast, and they's quick. Time you hit out at one, he ain't there, and another'n's bitin' your rump."

An extra sadness came into Ursa's usually cheerful voice. "My daddy, now, Ursa Major, he was all bear. But the hounds tuck out atter him, and him findin' it was like fighin' gnats, he clumb a tree. That's what a bear will do mostly every time. Then the man come along and shot him down, he did, and them hounds tore at his dead hide."

"Sorry," Cousin Frog said and afterwards thought how foolish it was to say anything.

"I was chased once my own se'f, and, knowin' a tree wasn't

no safe place to be, I tuck to a cave, a deep one. The man shot into it, but I was around a corner, and no harm done. The man he didn't have no stummick to come in, and the hounds hung back, savin' for one, and him I gave a love pat and didn't see him no more."

Abruptly Cousin Frog said, "When?"

"No time for more talk. I'm vamoosin'."

"I asked when."

"When what?"

"When does the man come back with his hounds?"

"Day atter tomorrow, the way I got it. That's two suns."

66

"Wait a day?"

"What fur?"

"Plans."

"You caught on to a plan?"

Cousin Frog had to say, "No."

"You shine, Tadpole, and I'm beholdin' to you, but here's a fix too mighty almighty even for your mind."

"Goodbye, then."

"No, hold on. I didn't aim to ruffle you."

"Goodbye."

"This ain't no way for us to part."

"It is. Can't trust me even for a day."

"Please git your dander down, Tadpole."

"You'd still have a start."

Ursa sighed again. It bothered him to think he had hurt his friend. "I'll trust you," he said. "Can't dock off more'n one day, though."

"Until morning, then."

"Till morning. Good-night."

Even this parting, Ursa thought as he turned to leave, was mighty short. Then it struck him with a feeling of relief that Cousin Frog wanted time to consider, time to figure how to get his old partner out of a fix.

When Ursa had gone, Amphibious, who had listened in a half-sleep, asked, "What's a hound, Cousin Frog?"

Cousin Frog didn't want to be bothered at a time when he must put his whole mind to a problem, but neither did he want to be curt with Amphibious. In the shallows of his mind he wished there were a short and satisfying answer. How describe a hound to one who had never even seen a dog? "Got four legs," he answered while his mind worked on Ursa's case.

"So have I."

"He bays."

"Bays?"

"Like Ursa grunts. A little."

"Does he grunt and run or run and grunt?"

"Both."

"Isn't that hard to do, both ways?"

"Bites, too. Now, hush, boy."

"Thank you for telling me what a hound is," Amphibious said sincerely.

Maybe it had not been so bad, answering childish questions, Cousin Frog thought. An idea had come to him, a glimmering of an idea. "Of all Pond Placid People, who are the safest?" he said more to himself than to Amphibious.

Amphibious was quick to answer, "I am."

"No."

"I'm never clear outside my house, and I can close it fast."

"Make it fast fast, huh? Go on to bed now. I must think."

At dawn Maggie Magpie came cawing by to see if Cousin Frog wanted any messages delivered. He told her to summon Mephitis Skunk and Needles the Porcupine. While he waited, he went over his plans, feeling secure and insecure. Had success, a couple of successes, gone to his head? Did he think he could do anything?

The idea, being impolite to Ursa and so getting him to stay another day! Putting him one day closer to danger! Maybe Ursa could have made it to the mountains ahead of hounds and hunter. One thing alone he knew: the scheme must work. But he hadn't even had it in his mind last night when he was rude to Ursa! It had to work.

When Mephitis and Needles came, he hardly knew what to say at first, so shaky did he feel. So he asked, "Feeling brave?"

Mephitis laughed, "Be prepared, that's my motto."

"And carry ammunition," Needles answered sleepily.

"I don't think I need to ask you how you feel about Ursa?" Cousin Frog said as a question.

"Fool questions bring fool answers," Mephitis replied, tickled because of what he thought was too-weighty an approach. "We hate him."

"Like a brother," added Needles, who liked to have things put right.

"Good. You'll have some fun, I think, and maybe just a pinch of danger. I'm going to talk to Ursa next, and later today he will tell you what we hope you'll do."

"No need to hope. We'll do it, eh, Needles?"

With that, the two safest people ambled away, cheerful and brave, but wondering.

Soon afterwards Ursa padded up. He said, rather gruffly because he couldn't altogether forget last night, "No miracles, I'm thinkin'. 'Bout to take off, I am."

Cousin Frog told him to sit down. They talked for a long time.

"You understand?" Cousin Frog asked afterwards.

Ursa replied, "The old game trail. I plant 'em. Run by. Hounds close."

"That's it." Cousin Frog found himself using Ursa's shortened speech. "See them. Rehearse. This afternoon."

Ursa voiced a rough "Awwg," by which he meant to show approval.

"If it weren't so far, I'd go with you."

"Now you set right around here, today and tomorrow. No cause to hop your heart out, I'm thinkin'." Ursa paused and took a deep breath. "Tadpole, hang your hide, this old cuss would bow down to you if he could bow that low. You're some!"

* * *

High in the heavens, so high that, seen from the ground, he was no more than a lost fleck in the sky, Scissorbill soared. With his eagle's eye he could see, even at that distance, all that sat or stood or moved around and in Pond Placid. Cousin Frog and Amphibious Turtle were together on the shore. Busy Beaver swam with a sapling in his mouth, making a broad wrinkle in the water. The Muskrats were just coming out of their house. Maggie Magpie was flapping around and cawing no doubt, a matter that sound, being slower than sight, would settle later. Needles the Porcupine stood by the old game trail, and farther along, toward the dam, stood Mephitis Skunk, both motionless. A short flight away from the pond a man walked, gun in hand, and three hounds sniffed around him. Now Maggie's cawing reached Scissorbill's ears.

He told himself, without feeling sorry, that he ought to feel sorry for those not so blest as he was, for those who were tied to the earth or the water or at best could make only shallow flights like those that Maggie made. Nature in her wisdom had put him apart from them. She had opened the world to him, to him alone, and he was not going to question her. She had put him beyond worry, beyond reach now of the man and his gun, leaving danger to the wretches who had to hide or to run. He had only to watch

Watching, he saw Ursa, hidden before, burst out of a thicket onto the old game trail, look for an instant toward the man and

71

the hounds and start running hard from them in his lumbering lope. The hounds, catching sight or scent of him, suddenly began to race, their noses close to the ground. After them the man pounded.

The pond quieted as if a hand hushed it. Busy Beaver dived. The Muskrats plunged into their house. Maggie flapped to a distant perch. Except for the still forms of Cousin Frog and Amphibious, the pond might have died.

And now Scissorbill knew why, for to his ears came the crazy, hoarse baying of the hounds. He slanted lower, the better to see the chase.

Ursa lumbered past Needles, making toward Mephitis, while the hounds gained. Then, strangely, Needles moved square into the

trail, his rear toward the oncoming pack. A hound sprang on him, open-mouthed, and Needles' tail slapped up, and the hound rolled away, pawing wildly at a muzzle frosted with quills. His running mates held up for an instant, then circled round. Almost lazily, Scissorbill thought, Needles moved out of sight into the bushes. The man kept on at a trot.

It wouldn't be long now, Scissorbill figured. The two hounds were gaining, gaining more as Ursa tired. Ursa went by Mephitis as if unseeing. Then, strangely again, Mephitis stepped into the trail, hind end to the heedless hounds. At a remove of three jumps he let them have it. One staggered aside, blinded, Scissorbill knew, and tried to clear his eyes on the grass. But one went on, and the

man, too, after Mephitis had eased himself into the brush. The man stopped as if to shoot and ran again, thinking better of it.

No matter. It was as good as all over for Ursa, running winded and awkward now, his fat jiggling loose to his lope. Goodbye, Ursa Minor. Goodbye, you old stumblebum. No more mountains for you. No more Pond Placid. Goodbye.

Of a sudden, beyond his thought, something got hold of Scissorbill. Something thrust into him like a pain, like a stab of joy, like something he didn't know what.

He didn't think about it. He couldn't. His wings bore him down of themselves and banked him hard in a curve behind the man and threw all the force of his speeding body at the back of the man's head. Before his wings could get going well again, he saw that the man had fallen.

He flew up and away and turned and saw the man rising and then examining the rifle he had broken in his fall.

Below and ahead of Scissorbill the last hound slashed at Ursa's heaving flank. As if with a last and utmost effort, with a speed hard to believe, Ursa switched around and batted him with his great paw. The hound sailed into the bushes, howling, and after a while began limping after his master, who waited and turned and started away with his broken rifle and his wounded hounds, as if glad to leave Pond Placid forever.

It wasn't until then that Scissorbill realized how bruised his chest was.

* * *

Later all the people of Pond Placid gathered at Cousin Frog's bank, and Needles and Mephitis and Ursa told the story, giving due credit to Cousin Frog, while Scissorbill perched silent on a branch.

After they were through, after everyone knew about the plan and its working out, Cousin Frog looked up at Scissorbill. He meant all that he did and said when he raised a hand and spoke. "We salute the King of Birds." And they all did salute him.

The King, still sore in the chest, descended stiffly to the ground. His voice was hoarse and halting. "Well — I — well — you see — well, we have to stick together."

He had never felt so good in his life.

* * *

Nothing would satisfy Ursa but that he show his appreciation. But what could he do? How would he show it? It struck him then that the most he could manage — the most and the most difficult — was a song first in praise of Cousin Frog but of Needles and Mephitis and the King of Birds, too. But he wasn't a poet! He could sing all right, he thought, but finding the words was a sight too much for an ignorant mountain bear. Since he could not go to Cousin Frog for help, because the song was in his honor, he went to Busy Beaver.

Busy didn't think, really, that the words Ursa already had thought out were too bad. Pretty good, in fact. Only here and there did he make a small change. And he didn't try at all to correct Ursa's language. Cousin Frog might educate Amphibious, but Ursa was a grownup and had a way of speech all his own, a way that fitted him.

So one night, in a fine baritone, Ursa sang to the people of Pond Placid:

Cousin Frog don't look like much,
Don't look like much,
Don't look like much.
His bald skin's chilly to the touch,
Yup, to the touch,
Yup to the touch.

He looks up yander day by day,
Yes, day by day,
The livelong day.
His thoughts seem fur too fur away,
Too fur away,
Too fur away.

But when it comes to savvy, he,
To savvy, he,
To savvy, he
Knows more than altogether we,
Together we,
Together we.

Of spunk he's got a fat galore,
A fat galore,
A fat galore.
We're glad to grant that much fur shore,
That much fur shore,
That much fur shore.

Skunk, King and Needles, take a bow,
Please take a bow,
Please take a bow.
They fit a fight, that trio now,
That trio now,
That trio now.
And rate a hand we'll all allow.

So, Then

After spring's splendor
And summer's surrender
And fall's fruitful show,
Winter comes wailing — and so?

The Last Leaf Shindig

Ursa Minor had the idea — to hold a fall festival or, as he called it, a "last-leaf shindig." No banquet, he said. Just an autumn singing and dancing in the woods, maybe under the tree where G. H. Owl had roosted.

It seemed fitting. The days were shorter and colder now as the sun swung south, making dawn come late and darkness early. When the wind blew, as it did more and more, the last of the cottonwood and aspen leaves shivered down, and some of them, curled, sailed like tiny boats on the troubled waters of the pond. The small nests of small birds, once hidden by foliage, came plainer and plainer to view, like secrets laid bare. On the slopes up from the pond the grass had seeded and given up and turned tan, and it wrinkled to the breezes like a worn and fallen banner. Mollie Cottontail, finding it as dry and flavorless as dirt, changed her diet to seeds and bark and the hips of wild roses that clung red to now-naked twigs. On the high peaks so far to the west that only Scissorbill and Ursa knew much about them, snow dazzled the eye when the sun shone and reached down, chilly-fingered, when it didn't.

Cousin Frog and Amphibious rose much later than before, lying numb until the sun warmed them and gave life to their limbs and falling dead to the world again when it cooled.

Amphibious, who never had gone through a winter, could not understand. "Are we dying, Cousin Frog?" he asked in drowsy concern.

Cousin Frog answered, "Nature will tell you."

"Whether we're dying? Do we just lay here?"

"You mean lie."

"Do we just lie here then?"

"You will know what to do. Nature will say."

Amphibious asked, "Out loud?"

"No."

"But how will I know?"

If Cousin Frog hadn't felt so listless, he would have tried to explain. All he said was, "You'll know."

Amphibious murmured, "Thank you, Cousin Frog," and closed his eyes and at the edge of sleep wondered what Nature was

Had he seen her or heard her when he was flung up to see the
world, in a time that seemed far away now?

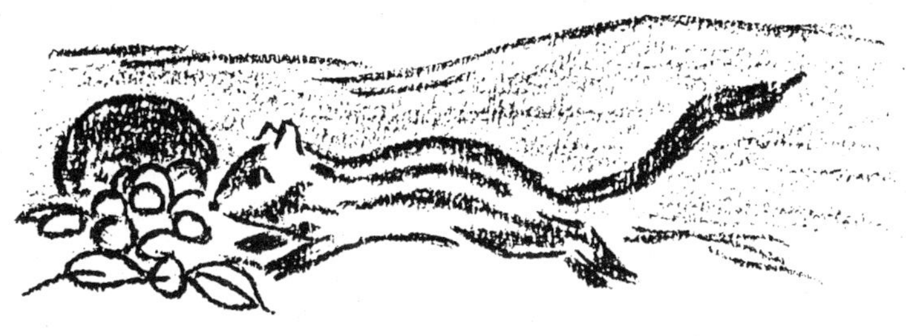

Over everyone there hung the sense of change, the sense of
coming partings, of different and separate ways of life. Tommy
Chipmunk counted his store of chokecherry seeds, laid by for the
time he would rouse from his sleep and need food. Busy Beaver
took stock of his saplings and told himself he surely had enough,
even if his household increased. Ursa yawned more and more and
felt of his fat, hoping he could live on it until spring, when he'd
come from his cave, lean as the hounds that had chased him,
hungry enough to bolt down a bug. Mousie Muskrat made a
nervous survey of the reeds close by his house. Mephitis told his
wife it would be a long time between eggs. Maggie knew she would
have to range far for food and wished she had Scissorbill's wings.
As if in proof of what was to come, as if almost to shame them for

their lack of spirit, the winter birds arrived, the downy and the hairy woodpeckers, frisky with purpose, and the black-capped and mountain chickadees, who kept piping gayly, "Chickadee-dee-dee."

But there surely remained time, time for the shindig, for the singing and dancing, for the last, glad, sad fling in remembrance of days gone, for a fleeting defiance of winter, for merry if haunted goodbyes.

So the invitations went out, carried by Maggie, who had to coax Blow Nose Badger from his hole and insist that everyone wanted him; and all of them met under Owl's one-time tree. It had

82

taken them time, though, for Cousin Frog's hops were short and slow, and Amphibious's pace was slower yet. For once he wished he could unload the weight of his house.

But the occasion gave spirit to them all, the occasion and the warming sun, which came out from under a cloud bank as if to watch and boost the fun. They sang the songs made up by Cousin Frog and Busy Beaver, and Ursa started on his solo, only to be joined by the voices of the rest, only to find himself capering to the time, as all of them did, one by one, while Maggie, overhead, beat out the rhythm with flappings of her wings.

All of them danced, that is, except for Cousin Frog and Amphibious, who weren't up to such exercise. Motionless, with his head half drawn in, Amphibious wished he could put words to a song, but all he could think of went:

> *When I lie me down to rest,*
> *I lay there like a log,*
> *And, resting, think how I am blest,*
> *With thanks to Cousin Frog.*

But those, he knew, weren't words for dancing but for sleeping, and, besides, something about them bothered him. Something about them would bother Cousin Frog. So he kept still.

The lines went out of his head when Busy Beaver started teaching the company a song that had just come to him.

Dance, all hands, dance.
Dance, join hands, prance.
Yes, we'll all get together
Whether here or wherever
Or whatever be the weather
To dance, prance, dance.

Having learned the song, they went to dancing again. The tune was light, fast, happy, and the company stepped and jumped

and pounded to it, their voices rising, as if each line were better
and merrier than the last. Over and over they sang the words.
Amphibious watched while sleep grew on him. Ursa kept leaping
high and wide, faster and faster, careful only not to step on the

smaller ones. The chipmunks frisked about, their tails flirting madly. Busy Beaver and his wife ran little circles while their tails drummed on the earth. Scissorbill, awkward afoot, thumped up and down, the Muskrats minced at the edges. Mollie was a smooth flow of motion. Mephitis cavorted crazily at the side of Mrs. Skunk and then, laughing, rolled over and over and found his feet and again started whirling and jumping as if he had never left them. Even Needles and Blow Nose, the slow pokes, got the fever.

> *Dance, all hands, dance.*
> *Dance, join hands. . . . .*

Mephitis went to sleep.

Warm with exercise, caught up in the fun, the furred and feathered folk hardly noticed a change in the weather, hardly saw or felt that the sun had died and a cold wind sprung up which spit a fine snow. But as they paused for breath Ursa asked, "How's that for hi-jinks, Tadpole?" and received no answer. A moment's hush fell on them all.

Ursa hurried over. "Cousin Frog! Hey, Tadpole! Amphibious!" He might as well have been speaking to the dead.

He put a paw on Cousin Frog. Gently he turned him on his back, without getting any sign of life. Then a hoarse, breaking roar rose in his throat. "Hang me! Oh, hang me! Colder'n a stone. While we capered, he friz, him and Amphibious. And it was all my idee. I wisht the hounds had got me."

They had all crowded around. From among them came Busy Beaver. Without speaking he stretched his warm body over Cousin Frog and Amphibious. He supposed they could freeze to death, uncovered as they were. He didn't know. All he knew was that frogs and turtles wintered in mud.

Ursa's anxious eyes were on him. "Feel 'em twitch, we'll get 'em movin'." When Busy didn't answer, he added, "That's what men critters allow. Keep movin', come a killin' frost."

Again Busy Beaver didn't know. But if Ursa said it? If he had heard men say it? All at once he felt lonely and lost. Who was he to think? Who was he to say what to do? He was used to doing what Cousin Frog suggested, and where now was Cousin's Frog's thought?

"Break trail home then," he said to Ursa. "Plow the way. Snow's getting too deep for them."

As if silenced by shame and grief, Ursa set off on the path that led home, shuffling the snow to the sides. It was Scissorbill's idea to follow close, to flap his great wings low to the ground and fan the trail clearer. Behind Scissorbill, like a small imitation, went Maggie Magpie. Those who remained kept quiet, waiting on time, waiting on the slow minutes that would bring them the answer.

When the trail crew returned, Busy Beaver said quietly, "Maybe. They're beginning to move."

"Good," Ursa said but did not say more, as if the case allowed for just the one word.

After Busy Beaver eased his body off, Cousin Frog and Amphibious stirred but neither spoke. It was with a plain-to-see effort that Cousin Frog opened one eye.

"Get 'em movin'. Get 'em movin'!" Ursa commanded. "They'll die else."

Busy nudged both Cousin Frog and Amphibious from behind. They began creeping, so slowly they might have been

glued to the earth. Now Busy, now Ursa, now Mephitis urged them on with pats and pushes. By slow and short step and step they made progress.

But now the weather worsened. The gray sky came down like a frozen cloak, and the wind screamed, and the thickening snow piled in the trail, so that Ursa had to keep tramping it down. "Keep 'em movin'!" he said again and again.

It was no use. Nothing was any use. In a little while no words, no urging, no encouragement could get Cousin Frog or Amphibious to go on. They lay as unmoving as frozen pieces of clay.

A fit of near-anger seized Busy Beaver. He should have used his own judgment, not yielded to Ursa. "We should have carried them in the first place," he almost snapped in the bear. "We big ones." He turned to his wife. "Go home," he ordered. "It's getting worse."

"I can carry 'em both," Ursa told him.

"You break trail!"

Scissorbill stepped up. "I'll fly with Cousin Frog."

"No. He's a poet," Busy answered, not sure what sense he was making.

It was a mark of the new Scissorbill, of the new King of Birds, that Scissorbill asked quietly, "Amphibious, then?"

"All right."

Ursa said, "Take care! You got mean claws," and went to the front of the line to break trail.

Busy Beaver looked back. "Come along, Blow Nose. We'll need you." Then he cradled Cousin Frog against his chest and set off a little clumsily, using his tail to steady himself. Scissorbill already was in the air, holding Amphibious in one foot.

At the pond Busy said, "Get to it, Blow Nose. Dig a trench right on shore, right in the muck."

Blow Nose dug it with only a few scrapes, dug it, Busy hoped, deep enough but just deep enough. Into it he laid Cousin Frog and Amphibious and had Blow Nose cover them over.

"Like a buryin'," Ursa kept grieving. "Like a dog buryin' a bone. Like men critters buryin' their dead."

"Do you die," Busy asked though he wasn't sure that one case proved the other, "do you die when you sleep the winter through in your cave? Does Blow Nose die in his hole?"

"But we're warm. Not iced up in a mud bank."

"But that's the way of them. That's what they would choose. We'll hope for the best."

So it was over, the fall festival, the last-leaf shindig, the singing and the dancing — and the burying.

"I'll go hunt my hole," Blow Nose said and departed without a goodbye. "Time we holed up, too," Tommy Chipmunk told his wife. One by one they departed, Scissorbill, Mollie, Maggie, Needles, Mephitis and wife, until only Ursa and Busy were left.

"Nothin' else for it, I reckon," Ursa said emptily. "Nothin' but to foot it to my cave."

"Nothing else."

"But I ain't happy."

"Try to cheer up. You don't understand our winter ways in the pond. See you next season." Busy added, as much for his own comfort as for Ursa's. "We all will."

"That I hope," Ursa answered, almost as if it were too much to hope. "So long, Chisel Tooth."

When his big shape was lost in sight in the sweeping snow, Busy dived into the pond and swam toward home. His wife would already be there, anxious to know how things had turned out.

For A Little While, Goodbye

Pond Placid is a place we know,
Though covered now by ice and snow,
And company we used to keep
Is mostly quiet or asleep.

Amphibious and Cousin Frog
Rest dumb and numb in shoreline bog;
And Busy Beaver, wanting bark,
Feels for his woodpile in the dark.

Here in the snow is Molly's track,
Here to a withered bite and back,
As lonely as the final sign
Of friends we counted yours and mine.

And Ursa, once so glad and brave,
Sleeps sad and helpless in a cave.
The Eagles claw tight to their cliff,
Their feathers fluffed, their pinions stiff.

There is no village news to tell,
So Maggie Magpie doesn't yell
Except to sound a dismal shout
If either of the Skunks comes out.

The melancholy days, we think,
The almost end, the very brink.
A wind comes up, hard from the east,
And calls the death of great and least.

The death? Don't ever believe it so,
No matter snow and ice and blow.
From wandering will come the sun,
Renewing life, reviving fun.